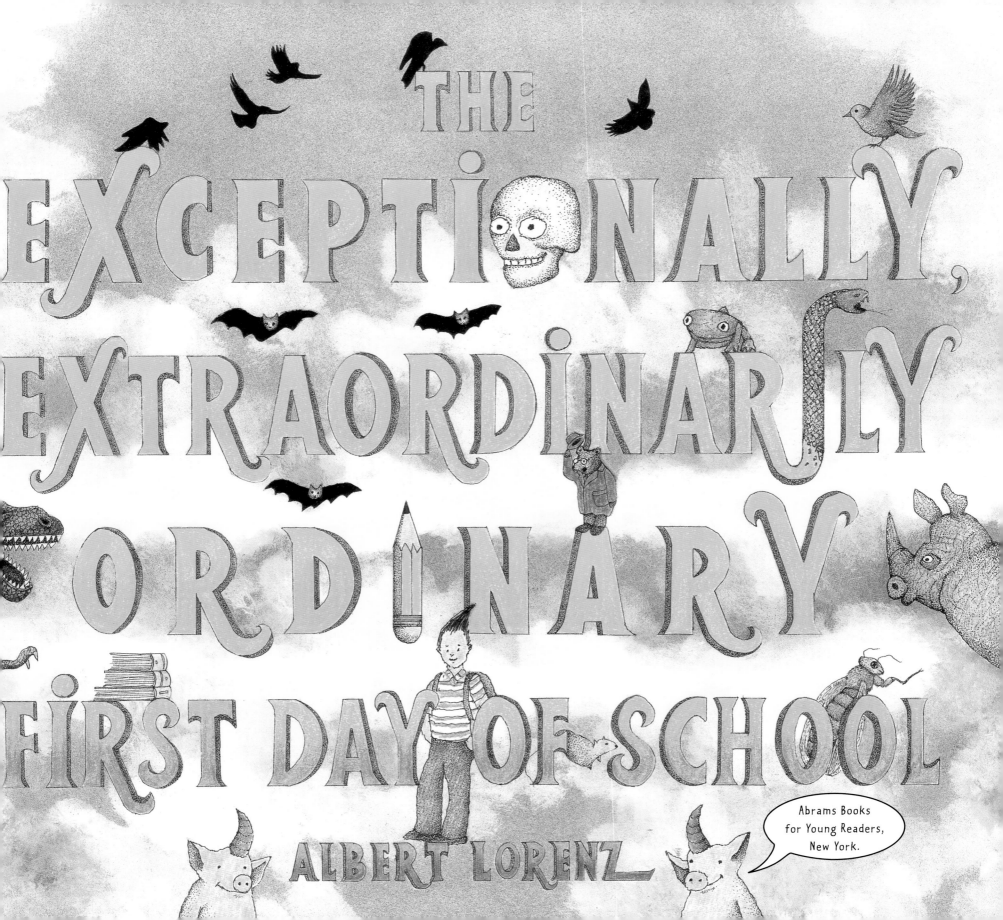

THE EXCEPTIONALLY, EXTRAORDINARILY ORDINARY FIRST DAY OF SCHOOL

ALBERT LORENZ

Abrams Books for Young Readers, New York.

"Welcome back to school, everyone," said Mrs. Dewey, the librarian. "What do you think about the new murals that were finished over the summer? Before we discuss them, let's all welcome your new classmate. John, where did you move from, and how do you like our school so far?"

"Well, I came from pretty far away. We had to travel down crocodile-infested rivers, fly in a hot-air balloon across a vast jungle filled with wild beasts, and then hire a car to get here," said John. "But I like it. It's ordinary enough. That is what my family is looking for: or-din-ary!

This is pretty similar to my old school, espec-ially after my uncle painted these murals."

Hmmm . . . I wonder why the murals just stay on the wall like that.

Extraordinary facts
Share these with your classmates, and you'll be the coolest person on the bus, on the playground, or in the hallway—especially on the first day of school.

Murals – Wall art. The only time you can paint on the wall and not get in trouble.

Kite – The Chinese invented the kite. That means they were telling one another to "go fly a kite" 2,800 years ago.

Pencils – The average pencil has enough graphite (the black stuff inside) to draw a straight line thirty-five miles long.

Paper – The major ingredient in spitballs. It was invented in China in the second century CE. Paper, that is. The spitball was invented soon after that.

Dewey Decimal System – The system created by Melvil Dewey for organizing library books.

Globe – Once people figured out that the world was not flat, they came up with a round map of the earth. You can spin it and pick out where you're going to live when you grow up.

But, Mom, I went to school last year!

"Did he?" asked Mrs. Dewey. "They seem so lifelike. Tell us, what was an ordinary day like at your old school?"

"Well, here I walk to school, whereas before I had to take the bus. It was always a rowdy scene."

Castle – They had moats, drawbridges, dungeons, and even toilets—primarily benches with holes in them, set in tiny rooms hanging off the "curtains" or outer wall. Watch out below!

Ravens – Fiendishly intelligent, glossy black birds. Often mistaken for crows and vice versa.

Edgar Allan Poe – An American author (1809–49) who wrote some of the scariest stories ever. He liked ravens a lot.

Concrete – A building material made of sand, cement, stone, and water. It has been around since the days of the ancient Egyptians. When they walked down the sidewalk, they avoided cracks because they didn't want to break their mummies' backs!

Hair gel – Check out the ingredients on your bottle. Noblewomen in medieval England used bird droppings and lizard fat.

Rhinoceros – Its horn is made of tightly packed keratin, the same stuff your hair is made of, so brush out your tangles or you might develop a horn.

Skull – The twenty-two head bones that protect your brain. But you still need a helmet.

"This place looks pretty new," continued John. "My old school was really, really old. And kind of a hangout for ravens. It could be sorta messy."

Welcome, chi

Welcome, children!

Welcome, children!

"Our teachers welcomed us on the first day of school, just like here. But sometimes they made us sorta nervous. All the growling and lip-smacking. There was always a kid or two who went missing—I mean, who didn't come back for day two."

"You mean they transferred?" asked Mrs. Dewey.

"You could call it that," said John. "We called it 'passing on.'"

"What kind of classes did you take, John?" asked Mrs. Dewey, with a puzzled look on her face.

lren!

Welcome, children!

Welcome, children!

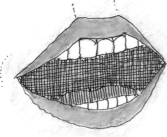

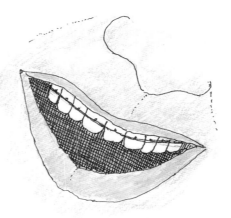

Lips – The things on your face that you use to kiss your dog.

Nose – The body part that yearns to have your finger in it.

Tongue – The licking muscle.

Facial hair – What boys aspire to and girls dread.

Fangs – Long, pointy teeth used to puncture. Some snakes have hollow fangs that inject poison into their prey.

Teeth – Brush these twice a day, or you'll end up like George Washington. He started loosing teeth in his twenties and had dentures made from gold, ivory, lead, and animal teeth (not wood).

Welcome – A greeting for people who come to your house. Unless they are vampires—then do not welcome them. Run.

Children – Small but extremely intelligent humans. Delicious, too.

Passing on – A nice way to say "pushing up daisies," or "kicked the bucket," or "eaten."

Frogs – Jumping amphibians that eat flies. And that have legs you can eat.

Parrots – Tropical birds that can learn to talk and are a pirate's best friend.

Bats – Nocturnal (that means they come out at night) flying mammals. Bats use sound to get around and find their dinner. Most do not suck your blood.

Skeleton – The 206 bones in your body that hold you up.

Flies – There are more than 300,000 kinds. Female houseflies lay 500 to 600 eggs in their lifetime of thirty days. Think about that next time you see a fly in your school cafeteria.

Rats – A type of rodent, officially called a large muroid. Rats rarely squeak in real life—all the better to sneak up on people sitting at their desks.

Hypnosis – You aren't actually getting sleepy. Hypnosis is a state of extremely focused attention.

Komodo dragon – They don't have wings and they don't breathe fire, but they're pretty scary. They grow up to ten feet long and will eat humans but mostly devour dead things.

"History was my favorite class," said John. "Mrs. Oldentimes said the best way to understand history was to meet and talk to the people who made it. She introduced us to a lot of people."

Time travel – The process that would allow you to go back to this morning and get the homework you forgot to put in your backpack before you went to school.

Easter Island – An island in the South Pacific full of huge carved statues called Moai. No one has seen a bunny or colored eggs on the island.

Sphinx – Half human, half lion, and full of riddles, the Great Sphinx is still standing in Egypt. The statue lost its nose to natural causes, by the way.

Great Wall of China – A giant wall built across China starting in 214 BCE. You can see it from outer space! Next time you don't want to drink your milk, remind your parents that the Chinese managed to build the Great Wall with very little dairy in their diet.

Can you find the following people from our past? Check out their history on the Web.

Genghis Khan
King Henry VIII
Benjamin Franklin
George Washington
Abraham Lincoln
Blackbeard
Sacagawea
Harriet Tubman
Queen Victoria
Napoleon Bonaparte

(Answers on last page)

Cymbals – Two metal disks that when smacked together make a loud, awesome, crashing sound. For the less experienced percussionist.

Baton – A thin stick used by a music conductor to keep musicians in rhythm. Also makes a good back scratcher.

Drums – The instrument you bang, the louder the better.

Wind instruments – Instruments like the flute that you play by blowing air.

String instruments – Instruments like the violin. The strings used to be made of sheep guts. Now they are made of sheep guts, steel, and nylon. Go figure.

Brass instruments – You pass wind through these metal instruments, but only by using your mouth.

"And what about the food in the cafeteria?" asked a kid. "Dee-licious!" exclaimed John. "Though sometimes sorta sad because we might eat what we studied in science that day."

"Computer class was pretty basic," said John.
"Just programming and stuff."

Computers – The first electronic computer was the size of a large room. Only giants had laptops back then.

Robots – Automated machines that sometimes act like humans. The ones in movies have more personality than the ones in real life.

Wires – Strings of metal that carry electrical impulses and your grandma's voice when she's calling you on your birthday.

Animation – The art form of making cartoons move.

3-D – "Three-dimensional," or how the world appears when we're looking around. Everything has depth.

2-D – "Two-dimensional," or how things look on TV—flat.

"During recess," continued John, "we would race horses, bungee jump, and parasail. It was great fun!"

Bungee jumping – An activity where you jump off something high with a huge rubber band hooked to your ankles. Screaming on the way down is acceptable.

Parachute – A fabric device that uses air resistance to slow the process of falling to earth. If you jump out of a plane, make sure you have one in your backpack.

Dizzy – What you are if you spin around too many times. Try it!

Parasailing – Being pulled by a boat so fast that your parachute lifts you off the water. Doing it over land is not very bright.

"Once a year we went on a field trip," said John.
"We went on one last year," said a girl sitting
nearby. "To the zoo."

Stars – Balls of gas far away in the galaxy that you can wish upon for some reason.

Moon – A spherical mass that orbits Earth. Other planets have moons, too. Sometimes more than one.

The moon is on average 239,000 miles from Earth (its orbit is sometimes closer to Earth and sometimes farther away).

LRV– A moon buggy actually called a Lunar Roving Vehicle (LRV) to make it sound very uncool.

Space suits – Pressurized outfits that astronauts wear to protect themselves during space exploration. If astronauts didn't have them, they'd be crushed by the pressure of the atmosphere. You can pee in them, too!

Nose picking – A favorite pastime everywhere. But remember to dispose of your boogers properly (not in your mouth, on the wall, under your desk, in your pencil box, into space . . .).

"Oh, that sounds like fun!" responded John. "We never went to places with animals or anything interesting like that."

Pointing your finger – Singling out or accusing someone or a group by aiming your finger at them. Especially useful if you smell a fart or notice an open fly. Also can be used to divert blame from yourself when accompanied with the statement "he/she did it" or the infamous "he/she made me do it."

Mouth hanging open – A sign of disbelief. Also handy for catching some of those 500 to 600 fly babies that just took to the air.

Sticking out your tongue – A rude gesture you make to express that you don't like something. It is just creepy when snakes do it.

Exit – The door to look for when art comes to life and a T. rex is on the prowl!

When school was out, John walked home, just like the other ordinary students. Though a lot of them appeared to be running pretty fast.

Gotta hang up. John's home from his first day at the new school.

"How was your first day, honey? Did they like Uncle Fresco's murals?" asked his mom.

"They did at first, I think. The librarian wanted me to tell everyone about my old school," said John.

"Did you tell her and the class what a nice school it was?" asked his mom.

"I tried, but Mrs. Dewey and the kids suddenly all ran away! Can't Uncle Fresco paint a still life sometime?"

Siblings – People who have the same parents as you do and are trying to drive you up the wall.

Parents – Old people who tell you what you can and cannot do. They often live in the same place as you, but don't have to. Sometimes there is one parent, sometimes two, sometimes more. And they all have something to say to you!

Home – The place where you live. And there's no other place like it.

Fresco – A painting on fresh, moist plaster.

Still-life paintings – Paintings of fruit, furniture, dead animals, and other ordinary stuff that doesn't move.

The illustrations in this book were made with pen and ink, watercolor, color pencil, and airbrush.

This book is dedicated to the memory of Joy Schleh, a consummate artist and true friend.
—A. L.

Cataloging-in-Publication Data has been applied for and may be obtained from the Library of Congress.
ISBN 978-0-8109-8960-3

Text and illustrations copyright © 2010 Albert Lorenz
Book design by Melissa Arnst

Printed and bound in China
10 9 8 7 6 5

Abrams Books for Young Readers are available at special discounts when purchased in quantity for premiums and promotions as well as fundraising or educational use. Special editions can also be created to specification. For details, contact specialmarkets@abramsbooks.com or the address below.

ABRAMS The Art of Books
195 Broadway, New York, NY 10007
abramsbooks.com

Answers for "people from our past."

1. Genghis Khan
2. King Henry VIII
3. Benjamin Franklin
4. George Washington
5. Abraham Lincoln
6. Blackbeard
7. Sacagawea
8. Harriet Tubman
9. Queen Victoria
10. Napoleon Bonaparte